D0579848

Here We Come!

written by
Janna Matthies

illustrated by
Christine Davenier

BEACH LANE BOOKS
New York London Toronto Sydney New Delhi

Here we come with a **rum-pum-pum.**

Wanna come?

Here we come with a rum-pum-pum,
and a **pick** and a **strum.**

Wanna come?

Here we come with a rum-pum-pum,
and a pick and a strum,
Little Lu on her thumb with a **swish-swish bum.**

Wanna come?

Here we come with a rum-pum-pum,

and a pick and a strum,

Little Lu on her thumb with a swish-swish bum,

fiddle-dee, fiddle-dum.

Wanna come?

Here we come with a rum-pum-pum,
and a pick and a strum,
Little Lu on her thumb with a swish-swish bum,
fiddle-dee, fiddle-dum,
clap-clap with a chum.

Wanna come?

Here we come with a rum-pum-pum,
and a pick and a strum,

Little Lu on her thumb with a swish-swish bum,

fiddle-dee, fiddle-dum,

clap-clap with a chum,

a **kazoo zum-zum.**

Wanna come?

Here we come with a rum-pum-pum,
and a pick and a strum,
Little Lu on her thumb with a swish-swish bum,
fiddle-dee, fiddle-dum,
clap-clap with a chum,

a kazoo zum-zum,
pop! pop! bubble gum.

Wanna come?

Here we come with a rum-pum-pum,
and a pick and a strum,
Little Lu on her thumb with a swish-swish bum,
fiddle-dee, fiddle-dum,

clap-clap with a chum,
a kazoo zum-zum,
pop! pop! bubble gum,
and a **drip** on a **drum** . . .

A drip on a drum?

Drip-drip on a drum,
drip-drip on a drum,
drippy-drip, drippy-drip . . .

Boom-Boom-
RUM-PUM!

Home we come!

Pop! pop! bubble gum,

a kazoo zum-zum,

clap-clap with a chum,

fiddle-dee, fiddle-dum,

Little Lu on her thumb with a swish-swish bum,

and a pick and a strum,

with a rum-pum-pum . . .

right back where
we started from.

What now?

Ho-hum. . . .

BIRDSEED

Some yum for the tum?

Here we come!

For my parents, who invited me into
the joys of music and poetry
—J. M.

For Pascale Taylor, my dear friend, my sister,
with whom I love spending summer nights
singing and dancing in the Lignerolles garden!
—C. D.

BEACH LANE BOOKS • An imprint of Simon & Schuster Children's Publishing Division • 1230 Avenue of the Americas, New York, New York 10020 • Text © 2022 by Janna Matthies • Illustration © 2022 by Christine Davenier • Book design © 2022 by Simon & Schuster, Inc. •

For information about special discounts for bulk purchases, please contact Simon & Schuster Special Sales at 1-866-506-1949 or business@simonandschuster.com. • The Simon & Schuster Speakers Bureau can bring authors to your live event. For more information or to book an event, contact the Simon & Schuster Speakers Bureau at 1-866-248-3049 or visit our website at www.simonspeakers.com. • The text for this book was set in Edwardian Medium. • The illustrations for this book were rendered in pencil and ink washes. • Manufactured in China • 1221 SCP • First Edition • 10 9 8 7 6 5 4 3 2 1 • Library of Congress Cataloging-in-Publication Data • Names: Matthies, Janna, author. | Davenier, Christine, illustrator. • Title: Here we come! / Janna Matthies ; illustrated by Christine Davenier. • Description: New York : Beach Lane Books, 2022. | Audience: Ages 0-8. | Audience: Grades K-1. | Summary: A boy sets off with his flute, his stuffed bear, and a rum-pum-pum, and making his way through the town and woods, he is joined by dancing and singing children and animals, one by one. • Identifiers: LCCN 2021003787 (print) | LCCN 2021003788 (ebook) | ISBN 9781534417878 (hardcover) | ISBN 9781534417885 (ebook) • Subjects: CYAC: Stories in rhyme. | Music—Fiction. • Classification: LCC PZ8.3.M442 He 2022 (print) | LCC PZ8.3.M442 (ebook) | DDC [E]—dc23 • LC record available at https://lccn.loc.gov/2021003787 • LC ebook record available at https://lccn.loc.gov/2021003788